Otherworldly Stories

Text by Tea Orsi

Illustrations by Isabella Ceravolo

whitestar kids

CONTENTS

WELCOME TO THE AFTERLIFE!

HELLO! YOU ARE AMONG THE PAGES OF A SURPRISING BOOK!

Soon you will leave on a truly special trip, an adventure that will take you to mysterious and fascinating places to discover where we may arrive after life.

Every civilization throughout history has had its own concept of the AFTERLIFE, and by reading the following pages, you will discover many of these INCREDIBLE STORIES. Some peoples thought that the soul reached an infinite grassland where the sun always shone, while others thought the soul landed in a dark kingdom without any way out.

Others actually imagined that the afterlife was a world similar to ours, but hidden and mysterious. You will read myths, stories, and legends from DIFFERENT LANDS AND CULTURES, which will try to answer two questions that we have always asked ourselves at least once: Where will we find ourselves when we are no longer here? And, who will we meet in the afterlife?

GET READY, BECAUSE THIS ADVENTURE IS ABOUT TO START!

THE KINGDOM OF HADES

ANCIENT GREECE

According to Greek mythology, the KINGDOM OF HADES is located underground and is a mysterious world, inhabited by many magical creatures.

HADES is divided into different areas: There is the RIVER STYX, which souls must cross to enter the kingdom, and the ELYSIAN FIELDS, a serene place where the souls of heroes and good people can rest in peace.

But there are also darker areas, like the TARTARUS, a frightening place where those who were mean in life are punished.

In this underground kingdom there is no sun, but there are lights that shine like small stars and illuminate the darkness, guiding SOULS; it is a place where life continues in a different manner, and there are many mysteries waiting to be discovered.

DESCENDING TO HADES IS A LITTLE LIKE TAKING A TRIP INTO THE UNKNOWN, WHERE, INCREDIBLY, MAGIC AND LEGENDS COME TO LIFE!

HADES AND PERSEPHONE

HADES, the god of the Underworld, has the same name as his kingdom. He governs with wisdom, assisted by his faithful companions, including PERSEPHONE, his queen, and has the task of protecting souls and making sure that everything goes well in this subterranean world.

HOW DID THEY MEET?

Their story is very interesting but also a little sad. One day while PERSEPHONE, daughter of DEMETER, the goddess of the earth and the harvest, was gathering flowers in a field,

HADES saw her and fell in love, so he kidnapped her and took her to his underground kingdom. Desperate because of the loss of her daughter, DEMETER stopped taking care of the earth, and so nature started to die. Nothing grew, the flowers did not bloom, and the harvest no longer arrived. The earth was sad without PERSEPHONE! In the end, ZEUS, the king of the gods, decided that a solution was needed. After much negotiation, it was discovered that PERSEPHONE had eaten pomegranate seeds while she was in the kingdom of HADES, and this action, unfortunately, meant that she had to remain with him for part of the year.

So, it was decided that PERSEPHONE would spend six months in the darkness of the KINGDOM OF HADES and six months on earth with her mother, DEMETER. When PERSEPHONE returned to the earth, nature became filled with flowers and fruit because DEMETER was happy to see her daughter again. But when she returned to the KINGDOM OF HADES, the earth became cold and uncultivated, and it was winter.

THIS STORY EXPLAINS WHY PLANTS DON'T GROW IN WINTER AND WHY, WHEN SPRING ARRIVES, NATURE AWAKENS AGAIN.

CERBERUS, CHARON, AND THE THREE JUDGES

In the Kingdom of Hades live some guardians. They have a rather scary appearance and maintain order in the afterlife. They are CERBERUS, CHARON, and the THREE JUDGES!

CERBERUS IS A GIANT DOG, WITH THREE HEADS AND A SERPENT'S TAIL.

He is the guardian of the KINGDOM OF HADES, and his task is to prevent souls from escaping from the underworld. If someone tries to flee, CERBERUS stops them with his frightening growl! GRRR!

CHARON IS A MYSTERIOUS FIGURE.

He is an old ferryman who takes souls across the RIVER STYX. The souls must pay an obol, a coin, to be able to get on his boat and reach the afterlife. If they don't have the coin, they must remain on the river's shore forever!

LASTLY, THERE ARE THE THREE JUDGES: MINOS, RHADAMANTHUS, AND AEACUS.

They judge the souls that arrive in the KINGDOM OF HADES and decide where they must go. Some go to the ELYSIAN FIELDS, a tranquil place for good souls, while the others end up in the TARTARUS, where only those who have done bad things are sent.

THE ELYSIAN FIELDS

The most desirable and serene area of the KINGDOM OF HADES is the ELYSIAN FIELDS. Imagine a large green meadow, full of green centuries-old trees and a sky that is always blue, without even one cloud.

IT IS A PLACE OF PEACE AND TRANQUILITY, WHERE THE SOULS THAT WERE GOOD AND FAIR DURING THEIR LIVES CAN REST AND HAVE FUN.

IT IS NEVER TOO HOT OR TOO COLD, BUT A PERFECT TEMPERATURE. FANTASTIC, RIGHT?

Those arriving in the Elysian Fields have lived with honor, courage, and goodness, like heroes or people who have helped others at all costs.

IT IS A PLACE WHERE THERE IS NEVER PAIN, ONLY HAPPINESS, FAR FROM THE PROBLEMS OF LIFE ON EARTH. IT IS AS THOUGH TIME HAS STOPPED HERE.

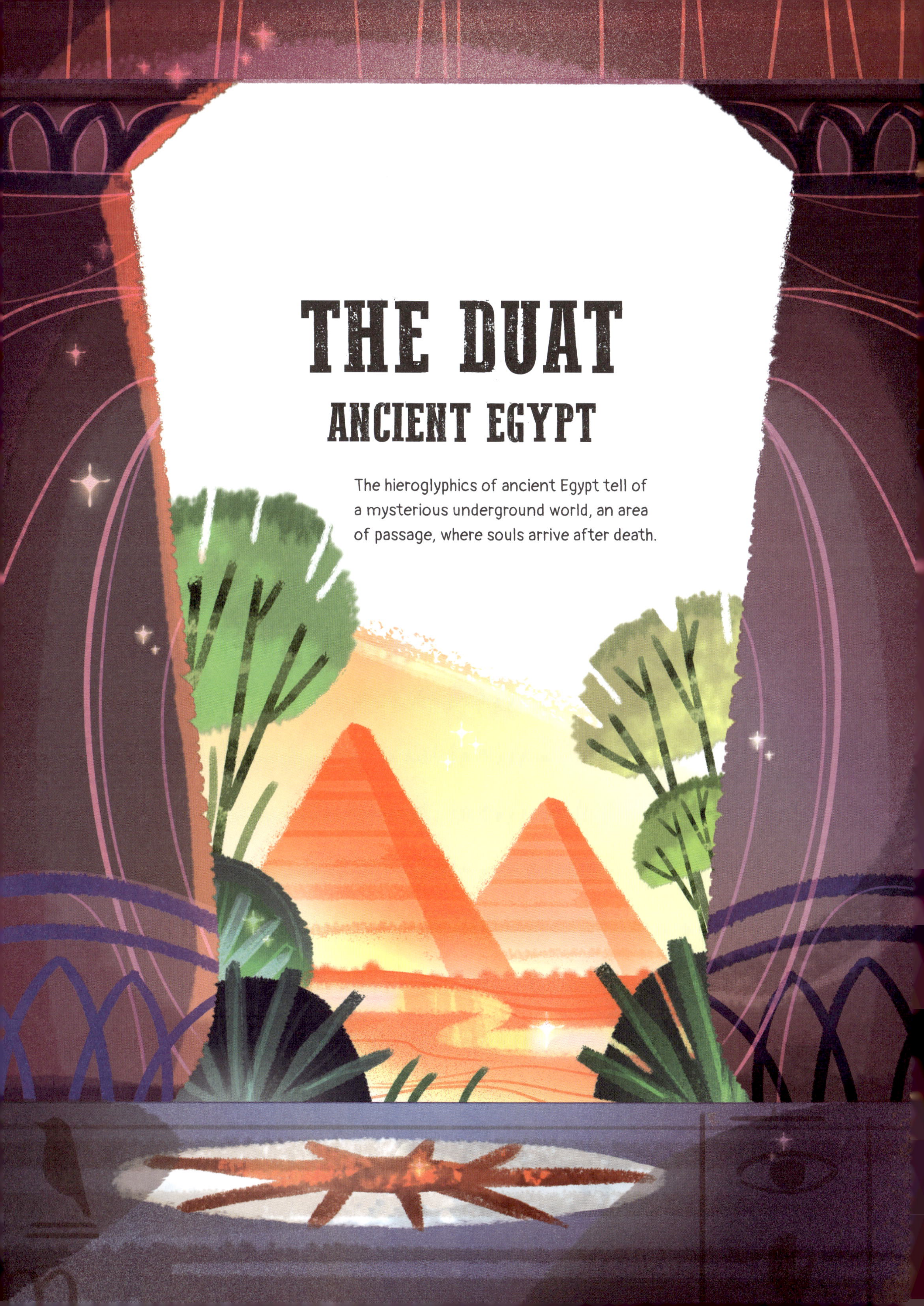

THE DUAT

ANCIENT EGYPT

The hieroglyphics of ancient Egypt tell of a mysterious underground world, an area of passage, where souls arrive after death.

ITS NAME IS SHORT AND EASY TO REMEMBER: DUAT.

It is a place full of mystery, divided into many areas, each with dangers and challenges that the souls must overcome to reach the FIELDS OF A'ARU, the paradise of the ancient Egyptians.

The souls must, in fact, overcome monsters and traps, and navigate rivers to arrive at the place where they will find eternal peace. The DUAT is not an easy place to visit, but those who manage to overcome the obstacles can finally live a serene life forever.

IT IS LIKE A GREAT VOYAGE THAT THE SOULS MUST ACCOMPLISH TO ARRIVE AT A SPECIAL PLACE, WHERE THERE ARE NO LONGER ANY WORRIES.

OSIRIS, ISIS, AND ANUBIS

Do you know the most famous deities of ancient Egypt?
You have certainly already read or heard their names:
OSIRIS, ISIS, and ANUBIS.

OSIRIS is the god of life, nature, and fertility. The ancient Egyptians adored him because he brought prosperity and food to everyone.
ISIS, his sister and wife, as well as goddess of magic and love, is very powerful and is always ready to help anyone who needs it. Then there is ANUBIS, the god with the head of a jackal, who has a very important job: He helps guide people in the DUAT.

OSIRIS, HOWEVER, DOES NOT HAVE A HAPPY STORY. I WILL TELL IT TO YOU HERE:

One day, OSIRIS'S evil brother, SETH, captured him and, to get rid of him and his power, put him in a box, which was immediately thrown into the NILE RIVER.
The box floated to a distant place, where a plant that grew around it became a large tree.

ISIS, who loved OSIRIS greatly and didn't know where he had gone, never stopped looking for him. She searched and searched until she found his body in that tree. At that point, with her heart full of love, she used her magic to bring him back to life, but OSIRIS unfortunately could no longer return to earth, so he became the god of the underworld.

According to the legend, ANUBIS helped ISIS mummify the body of OSIRIS, to prepare him for his long voyage to the afterlife.

SO, EVEN IF OSIRIS COULD NO LONGER BE WITH THEM, THE EGYPTIANS UNDERSTOOD THAT HIS SOUL WOULD ALWAYS WATCH OVER THEM.

THE WEIGHING OF THE HEART

In ancient Egypt, it was believed that after death the heart of the deceased should be weighed.

WHY? HOW? I WILL EXPLAIN IT TO YOU NOW!

A special ritual called the weighing of the heart was performed. The heart was placed on one plate of a magic scale, while on the other plate a feather of the goddess MAAT, who represented truth and justice, was placed.

To discover whether a person had been good and respected the rules, the heart had to be as light as the feather. If so, the person could enter the FIELDS OF A'ARU, where there were no more worries.

BUT IF THE HEART WAS HEAVY AND FULL OF LIES OR BAD ACTS, THE PERSON WAS TAKEN AWAY BY A HORRIBLE MONSTER WITH THE HEAD OF A CROCODILE.

This ritual was performed in front of many deities, including THOT, the god of wisdom, and ANUBIS, the god of mummification, who helped to guide the heart toward the scales.

THE FIELDS OF A'ARU

I have told you about the ceremony of the weighing of the heart and of the DUAT, so now you will want to know where the souls of the good people end up, those whose hearts are as light as a feather.

Well, they go to the FIELDS OF A'ARU. It is a wonderful garden, a place of peace and happiness where the souls of the good people can live forever. Here, everything is splendid; there are green meadows, majestic trees, and brightly colored flowers.

THE SKY IS ALWAYS CLEAR, AND THE AIR IS FRESH AND CLEAN.

In the heart of this paradise clear waters flow between rivers and tranquil lakes, where the souls can stroll along the shores or relax in the shade of the trees, loaded with sweet, succulent fruit.

AS YOU WILL HAVE UNDERSTOOD, IN THE FIELDS OF A'ARU THERE ARE NO WORRIES AND NO SUFFERING. IT IS THE IDEAL PLACE!

MICTLÁN AND TLALOCAN

THE AZTEC CIVILIZATION

In antiquity, the peoples who lived in Mexico were convinced that, after death, souls would arrive at an underground kingdom called MICTLÁN. The trip to this mysterious world lasted four years and required overcoming nine levels.

DO YOU WANT TO KNOW WHAT THEY WERE? HERE THEY ARE!

The first level was ITZCUINTLAN. Here, there was a river called Chiconahuapan, which could only be crossed with the help of the XOLOITZCUINTLE, the guide dogs.

The second, TEPECTLI MONAMICTLAN, consisted of crossing, at the right moment, the space between two hills that were constantly colliding.

The third was called IZTEPETL, and it was a hill covered in sharp rocks. Imagine how hard it was to cross it without hurting your feet!

Then, there were ITZEHECAYAN, the hills covered in ice, and PANIECATACOYAN, where the force of gravity did not exist and everyone could fly.

Afterward, one went on to TIMIMINALOAYAN, a path suspended in space and time, which led to TECOYOHUEHALOYAN, a place inhabited by ferocious jaguars.

Finally, one arrived at IZMICTLAN APOCHCALOLCA, where a river whose waters flowed black, carried the tired souls who had made it there and let them finally land in Mictlán.

WHAT AN INTERMINABLE TRIP!

MICTLÁN, however, was not the only world where the souls of those leaving their earthly life ended up. In fact, according to the Aztecs, there also existed TLALOCAN, a veritable paradise located in the sky, close to the sun. It was ruled by TLALOC, the benevolent god of the rain.

HOWEVER, ONLY THOSE WHO HAD DIED IN WATER, DURING FLOODS OR STORMS, COULD ENTER AND STAY HERE.

THE DAY OF THE DEAD

In Mexico, November 1st and 2nd are very important days, dedicated specifically to those who have left their earthly lives and now reside in the kingdom of the dead. It is DIA DE LOS MUERTOS which, in Spanish means "Day of the Dead." This holiday celebrates the deceased with gaiety, music, and many colors and is rooted in antiquity.

THE MEXICAN PEOPLE DECORATE THE STREETS, WEAR TRADITIONAL CLOTHING, AND PREPARE ALTARS WITH PHOTOGRAPHS OF THEIR LOVED ONES.

Following tradition, they also decorate them with PAPEL PICADO (tissue paper cut into shapes), yellow and purple objects to evoke life and death, candles to symbolize fire, and corn and cocoa seeds, symbols of the earth.

In addition, there are also some figures that are characteristic of this unique event, first and foremost LA CATRINA, the female skeleton who wears a large hat decorated with showy flowers and a stylish outfit. You have certainly seen many images inspired by her; each person decorates her as they wish, adding different, fun details!

Then there are also skeletons that are often depicted dancing and playing, and lastly, there is XOLOTL, a dog-headed god. This character, which was also one of the adored deities of the Aztecs, has the task of guiding the sun from the point where it sets to the exact place where it rises at dawn the following day. In the same way, XOLOTL guides the souls of the dead toward the afterlife so they don't get lost along the way. And yes, dogs are always man's best friends, in any form and also in the most unusual situations.

MICTECACIHUATL AND MICTLANTECULHTLI

Reading these words, maybe you think, who do these difficult names belong to?

WELL, VERY SOON YOU WILL FIND OUT. JUST CONTINUE READING!

MICTECACIHUATL and MICTLANTECULHTLI are the two Aztec deities that rule the kingdom of the dead.

MICTECACIHUATL is the goddess of death and protector of the souls, while MICTLANTECULHTLI is the god who presides over MICTLAN, the world where people go after dying.

TOGETHER, THE TWO DEITIES ARE MASTERS OF THE HEREAFTER AND HELP THE SOULS OF THE DECEASED DURING THEIR LAST, VERY LONG JOURNEY.

Both are often depicted as skeletons with great authority, but they also possess wisdom, since they have the task of supervising the balance between life and death.

VALHALLA AND ASGARD

NORSE MYTHOLOGY

The fearsome Vikings, who came from the lands of the north and sailed on ships with figureheads that looked like dragons, often spoke of the afterlife. Of all the places where their deceased could land after leaving their life on earth, VALHALLA was certainly the one most desired.

VALHALLA, in fact, was reserved only for the bravest warriors who had died in battle and were admired by everyone. It was a type of paradise and, if we want to be really precise, it was not really a world; it was a sort of enormous and majestic hall, presided over by the gods ODIN and FREYA.

YOU MAY BE ASKING YOURSELF WHERE SUCH A MARVELOUS HALL WAS LOCATED?

Here is the answer: in ASGARD, one of the nine worlds of the afterlife and the home of the most powerful individuals.

ASGARD is described as a beautiful place, with green meadows, high mountains, and a large palace, in which VALHALLA is located. These beautiful places were, however, deeply connected to the Viking concept of RAGNARÖK, which means "great battle."

The honored warriors who arrived in VALHALLA, in fact, trained every day to prepare themselves to fight the RAGNARÖK, which sooner or later would arrive. Their valor consisted precisely of this: They had been chosen after death to take part in the most extraordinary battle of all time.

NOT SURPRISINGLY, THE WORD "VALHALLA" MEANS "FIELD OF BATTLE."

ODIN AND FREYA

Odin is the king of ASGARD and the god of war and knowledge. He is very powerful but has only one eye because he sacrificed the other in battle to gain great wisdom. He also has two crows, HUGIN and MUNIN, that fly to gather information and bring it back to him every day.

In the large royal palace also lives FREYA, who is the sister of ODIN.

She is the goddess of love, beauty, and magic and is very kind to everyone but is also ready to protect what she loves at all costs.

She loves animals, in particular cats, and is famous for her chariot drawn by two magical cats who are very strong and fast.

IT IS SAID THAT ONE OF THE REASONS THAT FREYA LOVES CATS SO MUCH IS BECAUSE THEY ARE VERY INDEPENDENT, JUST LIKE HER.

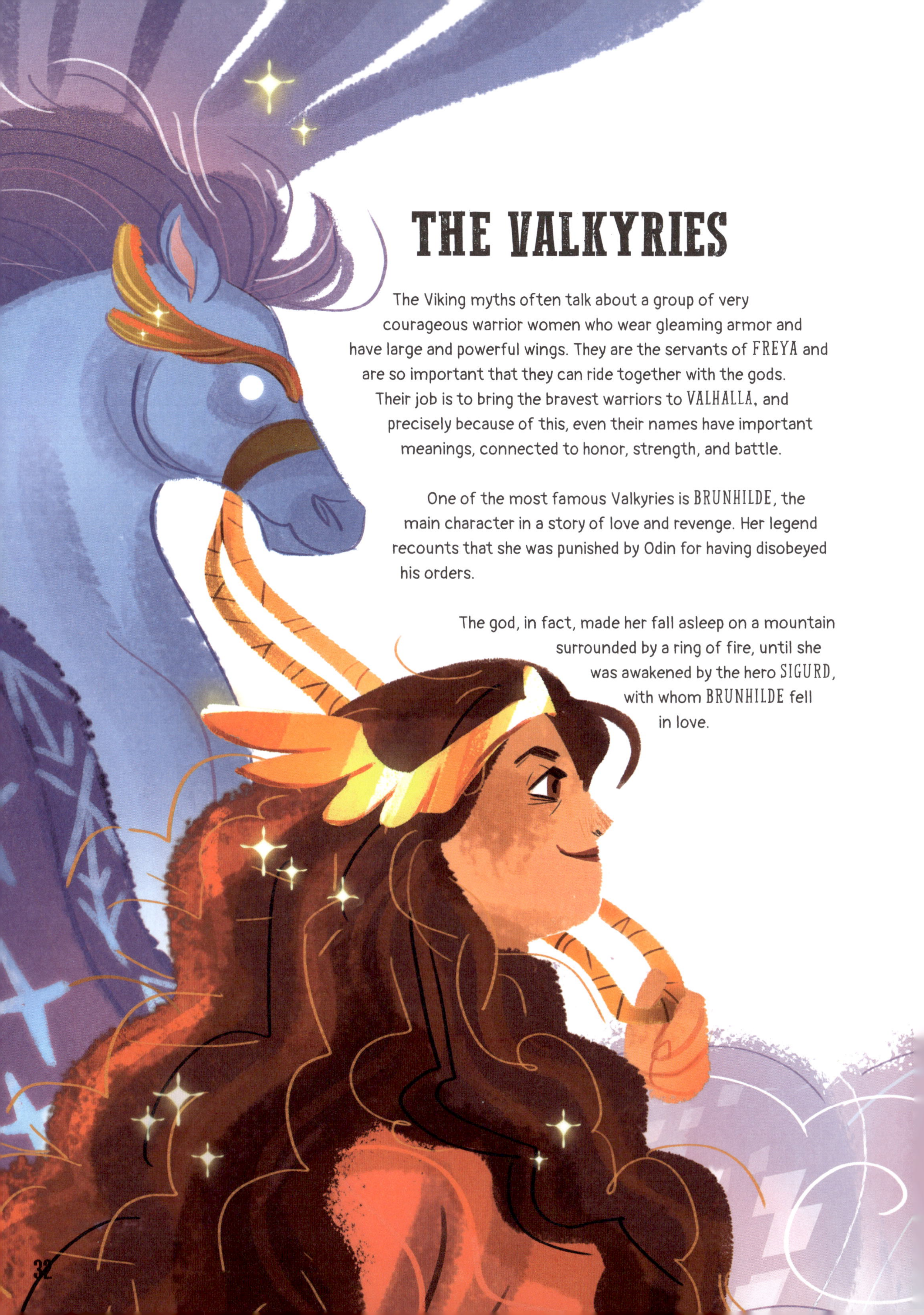

THE VALKYRIES

The Viking myths often talk about a group of very courageous warrior women who wear gleaming armor and have large and powerful wings. They are the servants of FREYA and are so important that they can ride together with the gods. Their job is to bring the bravest warriors to VALHALLA, and precisely because of this, even their names have important meanings, connected to honor, strength, and battle.

One of the most famous Valkyries is BRUNHILDE, the main character in a story of love and revenge. Her legend recounts that she was punished by Odin for having disobeyed his orders.

The god, in fact, made her fall asleep on a mountain surrounded by a ring of fire, until she was awakened by the hero SIGURD, with whom BRUNHILDE fell in love.

Another well-known Valkyrie is HILDR, who has the power to bring dead warriors back to life so they can continue to fight, creating battles that never ended.

Then there is GÖNDUL, who chooses the warriors who demonstrated the most honor and courage, deserving to go to VALHALLA. In fact, she represents justice and wisdom.

Finally, HERVÖR HALVITR has the capacity to change the destiny of the warriors thanks to her magic and her extraordinary powers. This Valkyrie also has a sister who often helps her; her name is HLAÐGUÐR SVANHVÍT.

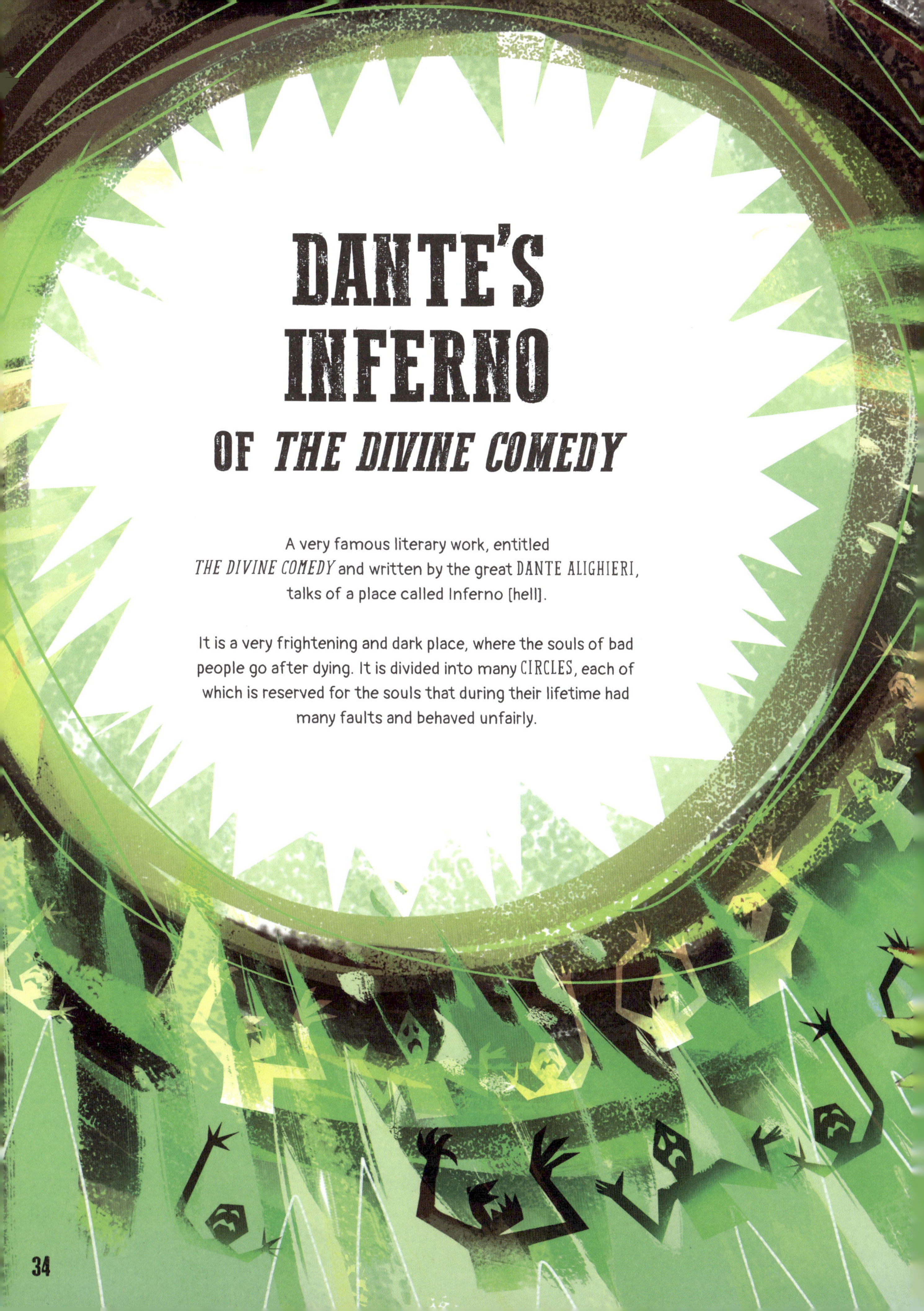

DANTE'S INFERNO OF *THE DIVINE COMEDY*

A very famous literary work, entitled *THE DIVINE COMEDY* and written by the great DANTE ALIGHIERI, talks of a place called Inferno [hell].

It is a very frightening and dark place, where the souls of bad people go after dying. It is divided into many CIRCLES, each of which is reserved for the souls that during their lifetime had many faults and behaved unfairly.

THE LOWER ONE GOES, THE WORSE THE SINS.

In fact, in one of these circles there are the MALEBOLGE, terrible places where the worst sinners are punished. The MALEBOLGE are divided into ten large *bolge*, or ditches, each with a different punishment.

AN EXAMPLE?

There is a *bolgia* where the souls of the BARATTIERI, or BARRATORS, who swindled other people, are immersed in hot, slippery mud, while others are punished by walking under rains of fire or buffeted by very strong winds.

DANTE'S GUIDES

In *THE DIVINE COMEDY*, DANTE takes a voyage from the Inferno to Paradise, and in order not to get lost, he needs very special and important guides.

I WILL INTRODUCE THEM TO YOU!

The first guide that DANTE meets is VIRGIL, a poet of ancient Rome, who represents reason and wisdom and accompanies DANTE through the INFERNO and PURGATORY, describing to him the places that they visit and the punishments of the MALEBOLGE.

After the voyage through the Inferno and PURGATORY, DANTE méets a new guide: BEATRICE, a beautiful woman who represents love and salvation and guides him through PARADISE.

MINOS, THE CENTAURS, GERYON, AND THE MINOTAUR

During his voyage through the INFERNO, DANTE meets many strange, frightening figures. Each of these figures has a specific job in the Inferno, and their presence serves to demonstrate the severity of the sins and the terrible punishments that the souls must face.

HERE ARE SOME OF THEM:

MINOS is a great mythological king who lives at the entrance to the INFERNO. His task is very important: It is he who judges the souls and decides into which circle of the INFERNO they must go, depending on the sins that they have committed.

The CENTAURS are half man and half horse, and they are located in a circle of the INFERNO where violent souls are punished. The CENTAURS are always ready to shoot arrows and to fight.

GERYON, a creature with the body of a serpent and the face of a man, is the symbol of deceit. DANTE meets him when he has to descend from one circle to another.

Last, the MINOTAUR is a creature with the body of a man and the head of a bull. He represents violence, and DANTE sees him when he becomes agitated in his prison.

PURGATORY AND PARADISE

DANTE, after leaving the Inferno, arrives at two special and happier places: PURGATORY and PARADISE.

PURGATORY is like a big mountain that rises toward the sky, and here are the souls that want to purify themselves of the sins committed during their lives, to be able to enter Paradise.

It is divided into seven terraces, each of which is dedicated to a different sin that the souls must overcome but, unlike the Inferno, here they do not suffer forever.

AFTER HAVING BEEN PURIFIED, THEY CAN RISE TOWARD PARADISE, WHERE THEY WILL FIND PEACE.

PARADISE is the most beautiful place of all, where the souls go after having purified their sins. It is a world of light, where everyone is happy and lives in perfect harmony with everything around them.

DANTE RISES THROUGH NINE SKIES, WHICH BECOME INCREASINGLY BRIGHTER AND FULL OF JOY.

YOMI-NO-KUNI
JAPANESE MYTHOLOGY

YOMI-NO-KUNI is a special place often mentioned in Japanese mythology: the kingdom of the dead. It is an underground world that is a mysterious and dark, not bright like the world we know.

IN YOMI-NO-KUNI, THE PEOPLE ARE NO LONGER ALIVE, BUT THEY HAVE NOT COMPLETELY DISAPPEARED: THEY ARE LIKE SHADOWS THAT MOVE BETWEEN LIGHT AND SHADOW.

It is described as a sad and silent place, where the ground is damp and where there are no colors and nothing living grows, but what makes it most disturbing is that no one can return from there once they arrive.

YŌKAI

In Japan, since ancient times, many legends have been handed down that have protagonists with extraordinary powers. These creatures move on the boundary between reality and illusion and between life and death.

I am talking about the YŌKAI, spirits that can have a monstrous appearance or blend in with the common people, influencing their actions and thoughts.

INCREDIBLE, RIGHT?

In general, the YŌKAI go into action at night, maybe because in the dark their tricks become even more mysterious.

Then, among them there are the ONI, the YŌKAI that are the most terrible and strongest of all. They look like ogres or demons, are taller than the trees, and have bristly hair, and their skin is red, green, or blue. But that is not all: They also have horns, tusks, and very long claws. Their clothing is truly particular; they wear tiger skins and always hold large iron clubs in their hands.

WHY ARE THEY SO MONSTROUS?

Well, they are the guardians of the gates of hell and monitor those who live there, preventing them from getting out! No one dares to challenge them!

The ONI are so famous that there is a holiday that celebrates them.

JUST THINK THAT, DURING THAT EVENING, TO KEEP THEM FAR AWAY FROM THEIR HOUSES, FAMILIES ATTACH DRIED FISH HEADS AND BRANCHES OF HOLLY FULL OF THORNS TO THEIR DOORS!

IZANAMI AND IZANAGI

The story of YOMI-NO-KUNI is tied to the legend of IZANAMI and IZANAGI, two creation deities in the Japanese pantheon. When IZANAMI dies during the birth of a son, she finds herself in YOMI-NO-KUNI, where her form becomes a little frightening.

Desperate, her husband IZANAGI, who does not want to lose her, decides to descend into the kingdom of the dead to look for her, but when he finds her IZANAMI is changed and now does not look at all like she did before. She has become a horrible figure that strikes fear!

Seeing her, IZANAGI is frightened and runs away from YOMI-NO-KUNI, but while he is fleeing, IZANAMI curses him, saying that he will never be able to return to the land of the living.

To prevent her from following him, IZANAGI puts a large stone in front of the entrance of YOMI-NO-KUNI, sealing the entrance.

FROM THAT MOMENT ON, IZANAMI BECOMES THE GODDESS OF THE DEAD, AND YOMI-NO-KUNI REMAINS THE PLACE WHERE THE SOULS OF THE PEOPLE WHO DIE RESIDE.

TAKAMANOHARA

TAKAMANOHARA is the name of the sky in Japanese mythology, and it is a very special place where the gods live. It is located very high above the earth and is shining and perfect, filled with harmony and beauty.

IMAGINE IT AS A CLOUDLESS SKY, CALLED "SUPREME SKY," THAT IS ALWAYS BRIGHT AND WHERE EVERYTHING IS ORDERLY AND PEACEFUL.

IT IS HERE THAT THE MOST IMPORTANT GODS MEET TO MAKE DECISIONS ON THE DESTINY OF THE WORLD.

TAKAMANOHARA is also the place where the life and energy of the sky intertwine with that of the earth and where everything is in equilibrium. From here the gods observe the actions of human beings to protect and guide them. In this magical place, many of the most important stories of Japanese mythology begin, such as the creation of the world and the origins of the deities that populate Japan.

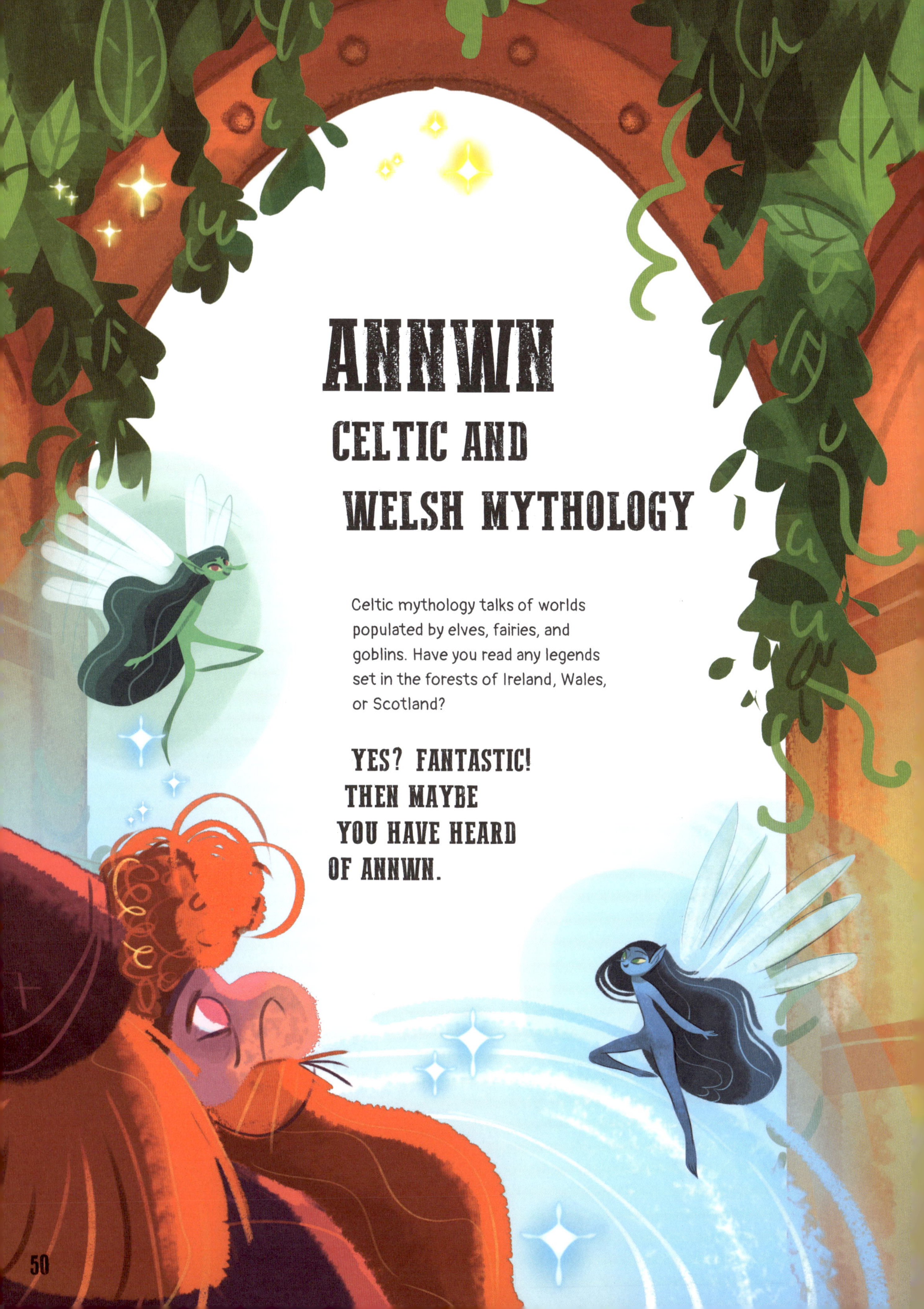

ANNWN

CELTIC AND WELSH MYTHOLOGY

Celtic mythology talks of worlds populated by elves, fairies, and goblins. Have you read any legends set in the forests of Ireland, Wales, or Scotland?

YES? FANTASTIC! THEN MAYBE YOU HAVE HEARD OF ANNWN.

WHAT IS IT?

Well, it is a truly special place that can be accessed by passing through a big gate. It is a little like another world, but mysterious and filled with magic. Imagine an enchanted island, where everything is beautiful and serene, a place where the people and creatures can live in peace and serenity ... for good!

It is like a large garden where there are no worries, only tranquility and happiness. According to the legends, ANNWN is located beyond our world, where time flows differently. Here there are heroes, courageous warriors, and deities who did great things during their lifetimes, defeating terrible monsters and carrying out impossible feats. After having experienced so many adventures, they arrive at this tranquil place, where they can finally rest and devote themselves to what they most like to do. ANNWN is also a mysterious world, where many marvels exist, like fantastic animals and hidden places that only the wisest can discover.

IT IS A LITTLE LIKE A DREAM, WHERE EVERYTHING IS POSSIBLE AND THE BEAUTY OF NATURE IS INFINITE.

THE MYTH OF ARAWN AND PWYLL

Now that you know about ANNWN, would you like to read a story set right there?

One day, a king named PWYLL, very courageous and wise but also very curious, was hunting in a forest and met a mysterious creature: a large white dog that seemed special and took him to a magic door that opened onto another world. Well, you must know that this world was in fact ANNWN, the kingdom of another king called ARAWN, who was very powerful but also a little solitary.

ARAWN, UNFORTUNATELY, HAD A BIG PROBLEM: HIS ENEMY, ANOTHER KING NAMED HAVGAN, CONSTANTLY CHALLENGED HIM BECAUSE HE WANTED TO TAKE POSSESSION OF HIS THRONE.

So, when ARAWN met PWYLL, he had a very cunning idea: He proposed they change places for a while! This way, PWYLL would be able to help him defeat HAVGAN, while ARAWN would live in PWYLL'S kingdom, enjoying a little tranquility.

PWYLL, who was a very courageous king, accepted without thinking too much about it. So, the two switched places: PWYLL became the king of ANNWN, while ARAWN took the place of PWYLL in his kingdom. Before leaving, however, ARAWN gave him very important advice: He must never laugh or be happy in the kingdom of ANNWN because every smile and every laugh could make the powerful creatures that lived in the kingdom angry. PWYLL, with his heart filled with courage, faced the battle against HAVGAN, and thanks to his strength and cunning, managed to defeat him. When he returned, the king of ANNWN congratulated him with great gratitude. The two friends changed places again, but PWYLL never forgot this incredible adventure.

FROM THAT DAY, ARAWN AND PWYLL WERE GREAT FRIENDS, AND THEIR BOND BECAME SO STRONG THAT THEY ALWAYS HELPED EACH OTHER, EVEN IN THE MOST DIFFICULT SITUATIONS.

CŴN ANNWN, DEMONS, AND MAGIC PIGS

In ANWANN, extraordinary creatures live, some marvelous, others a little more frightening, but all very, very fascinating.

HERE ARE SOME VERY IMPORTANT ONES:

There are magical dogs called CŴN ANNWN, with fur as white as snow and eyes red as fire. They are the guardians of ANNWN and follow their king, ARAWN, wherever he goes. They are so fast that they can run across the sky, and it is said that their howls are the sound of death approaching. But don't worry: They are not bad! In reality, they are friends that protect ANNWN and help to maintain order in the kingdom. Some people say that seeing them at night means that something magical is happening.

ANNWN is not only a beautiful and tranquil place but is also a world where there are mysterious creatures called demons. These demons are obscure and powerful beings that inhabit the most hidden places of ANNWN. Sometimes it is said that they create fear to protect the kingdom from those trying to get in without permission. Only the most courageous people can confront them without becoming frightened.

And then, there are the magic pigs! These pigs are not like those we see on the farms. They are special because they are enormous and equipped with extraordinary powers. Imagine that they are capable of producing endless food.

IT IS SAID THAT EVERY TIME A MAGIC PIG IS COOKED, ITS BODY RETURNS TO LIFE AND CAN FEED ANYONE, WITHOUT EVER RUNNING OUT.

PEKLO AND NAV

SLAVIC MYTHOLOGY

The legends belonging to Slavic mythology often speak of PEKLO and NAV, two very particular places linked to life after death and the world of the spirits.

BUT WHAT IS THE DIFFERENCE BETWEEN THE TWO?

PEKLO is a dark and scary place, similar to hell, where the souls of people who behaved badly in life go. It is a place populated by wicked creatures, such as evil demons and spirits, that torment lost souls—a sort of kingdom of the shadows, where pain and suffering reign.

NAV, instead, is a more mysterious and silent world. It is the kingdom of the spirits, a place that is located between life and death. In NAV there is no happiness, but also not great suffering. It is not a place of punishment, but a space where the spirits are condemned to wander for eternity, waiting to be forgotten.

BOTH WORLDS ARE CLOSELY TIED TO DEATH AND DESTINY, AND EACH ONE REPRESENTS A DARK AND MYSTERIOUS PART OF THE VOYAGE AFTER LIFE.

PEKLENK AND OZWIENA

WHO RULES OVER PEKLO?

PEKLENC is a very powerful god in Slavic mythology. Imagine a very astute and strong man of the shadows who can also turn into various animals, becoming a big bear or a serpent.

The legends set in PEKLO also speak of OZWIENA, the goddess of echo and gossip. When she was in PEKLENC's service, she had a very dark role: Her job was to convey to the living the frightening sounds of the damned as a reminder of what might await them.

NOW I WILL TELL YOU WHAT PEKLENC DOES IN PEKLO.

He has the task of judging the souls, deciding whether they can rest in peace or if they have to be punished. If a person has lived a good and fair life, the soul is left in peace, but if they have behaved unfairly, they are condemned to wander in the darkness of PEKLO, tormented forever. But remember one important thing: PEKLENC is not only bad!

Even if he can seem severe, he has a mission: He tries to maintain the balance between good and evil.

SOMETIMES, THE SOULS WHO MADE MISTAKES CAN LEARN FROM THOSE ERRORS AND MANAGE TO FIND A LITTLE PEACE.

THE CREATURES OF PEKLO AND THE CHALLENGES OF GETTING IN

Peklo, like the other worlds that you have already learned about in this book, is populated by monstrous creatures.

One of these is the THREE-HEADED DOG that protects the entrance of this dark kingdom. Its three heads growl and drool poison, ready to defend the entrance against anyone who dares to come close without permission. In the SMORODINA RIVER, which flows close by, live poisonous creatures such as serpents and dragons, ready to bite anyone who comes too close. In the shadows, there is also the gigantic guardian dragon that flies over the waters to protect the hidden secrets of PEKLO.

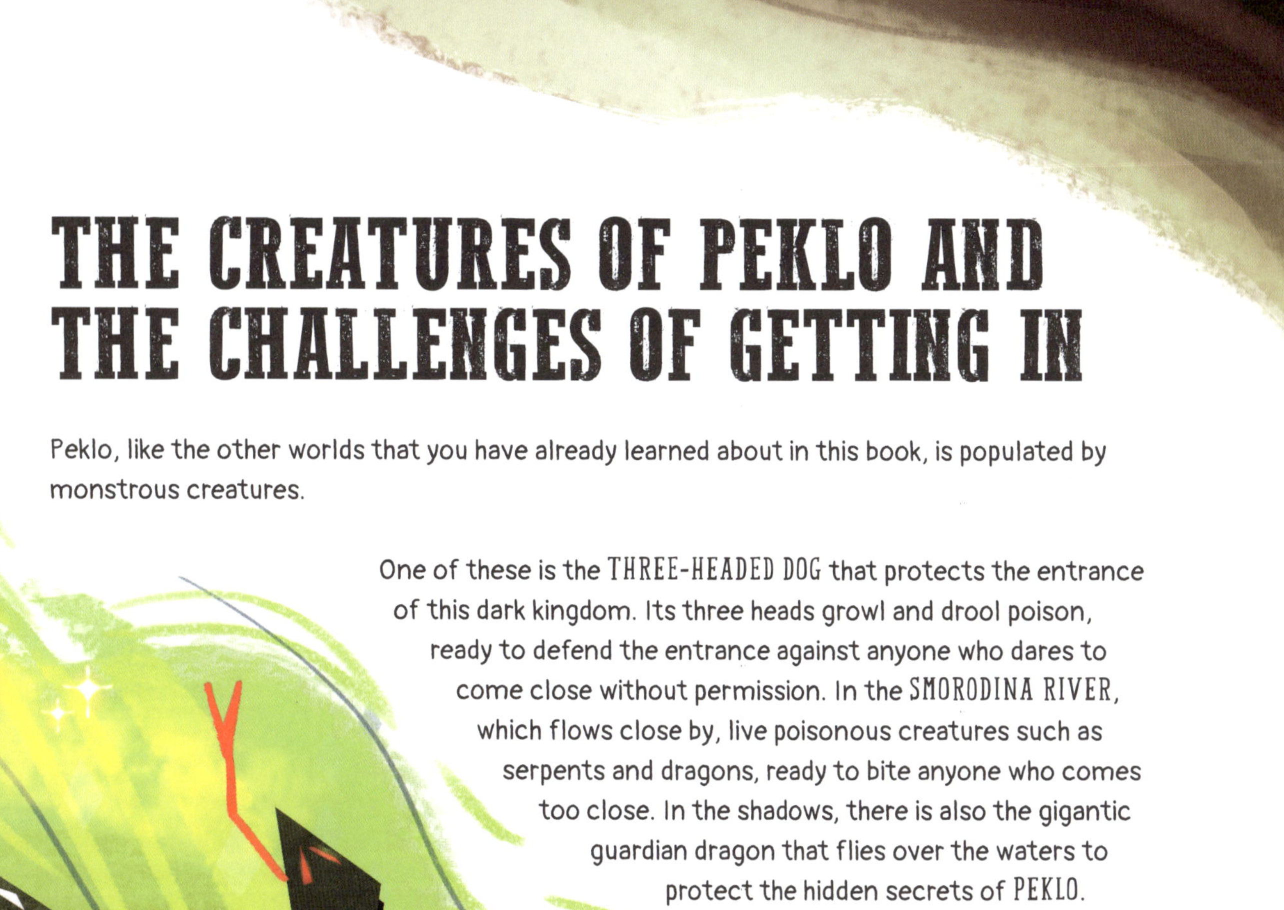

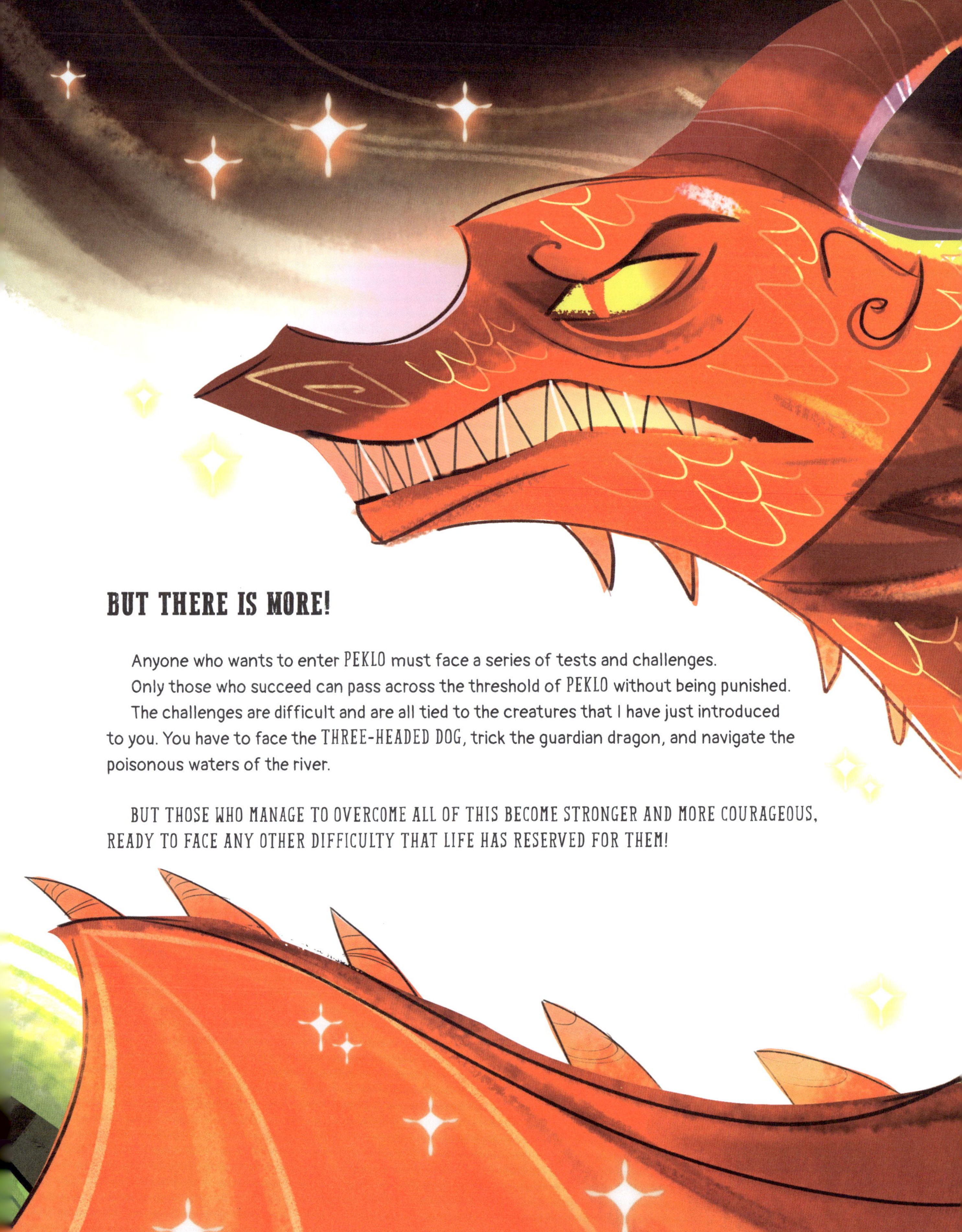

BUT THERE IS MORE!

Anyone who wants to enter PEKLO must face a series of tests and challenges.

Only those who succeed can pass across the threshold of PEKLO without being punished.

The challenges are difficult and are all tied to the creatures that I have just introduced to you. You have to face the THREE-HEADED DOG, trick the guardian dragon, and navigate the poisonous waters of the river.

BUT THOSE WHO MANAGE TO OVERCOME ALL OF THIS BECOME STRONGER AND MORE COURAGEOUS, READY TO FACE ANY OTHER DIFFICULTY THAT LIFE HAS RESERVED FOR THEM!

TUONELA

FINNO-UGRIC MYTHOLOGY

According to the ancient Finnish stories, there is a distant place called TUONELA, a mysterious underground kingdom, where the souls of those who have departed this world live.

BUT DON'T THINK IT IS A DARK, SAD PLACE!

It is a mysterious place, but also full of beauty and magic, where every soul finds peace. TUONELA is crossed by a very special river, the TUONELA River, which flows with waters that are dark as night. It is said that this river separates the world of the living from that of the dead, and whoever tries to cross it must be very careful! It can seem like an impossible mission, but those who are really courageous can succeed.

THERE IS ANOTHER ASPECT THAT MAKES THIS KINGDOM SPECIAL!

The legends say that there is very beautiful music playing in the kingdom, a soft and mysterious melody that can only be heard by those who have a pure heart. It is said that this sound comes from the heart of TUONELA, and those who manage to hear it can understand the secrets of the universe.

THE MYTH OF TUONI AND TUONETAR

TUONELA is ruled by King TUONI, the god of death, and his wife, TUONETAR.

TUONI is a mysterious, powerful figure who has the task of governing all the souls who arrive in the kingdom of the dead, but he is not bad. His task is to give a new beginning to the souls who have arrived in his kingdom. His wife TUONETAR also takes care of the souls and represents the underground land. Her beauty is often compared to the calm and serenity that reign in the kingdom of the dead, and she is known for having great strength and a kind heart.

BUT HOW DID THEY MEET?
HERE IS THEIR STORY....

A long time ago, TUONETAR lived alone in a very distant place, in the kingdom of the shadows. One day, she felt that her heart was filling with sadness, as if something was missing. So, she decided to descend into a deeper place, where the sky met the earth and where the waters flowed slow and cold. While she was walking, she met TUONI, who already reigned over TUONELA. He asked her, "Why are you so sad?"

TUONETAR answered, "I feel as though I am not complete. Something is missing ... maybe someone." TUONI, who for some time had been reigning over TUONELA alone, approached her and with gentleness said, "I am alone in this kingdom and you seem to understand the solitude. Maybe together we could reign over TUONELA, bringing to life our kingdom of peace."

TUONETAR accepted and from that day became the companion of TUONI. Together they reign over TUONELA, the mysterious kingdom of the dead, where all souls are welcomed with respect and tranquility.

TUONEN TYTTI, THE BLACK SWAN, AND KALMA

In the mysterious kingdom of TUONELA live various fascinating creatures.

HERE ARE THE MOST IMPORTANT:

TUONEN TYTTI is a beautiful young woman who takes care of the souls and helps them find their place in the kingdom of the dead. She is a kind, protective figure and the guardian of the gates of TUONELA. She is also very brave and is not afraid to stay among the shadows because, for her, death is simply a passage toward a tranquil world.

The BLACK SWAN is a majestic bird that flies over the dark waters of the TUONELA River, bringing the souls toward eternal rest. Its shiny feathers symbolize the beauty and sadness of death, and its silent, elegant flight is a sign of peace and infinite serenity.

KALMA, instead, is the goddess of death. She represents the return to earth and the cycle of life that continues even after death. Her body is covered by withered flowers and dry leaves because she represents the end of a cycle of life, but also the beginning of another.

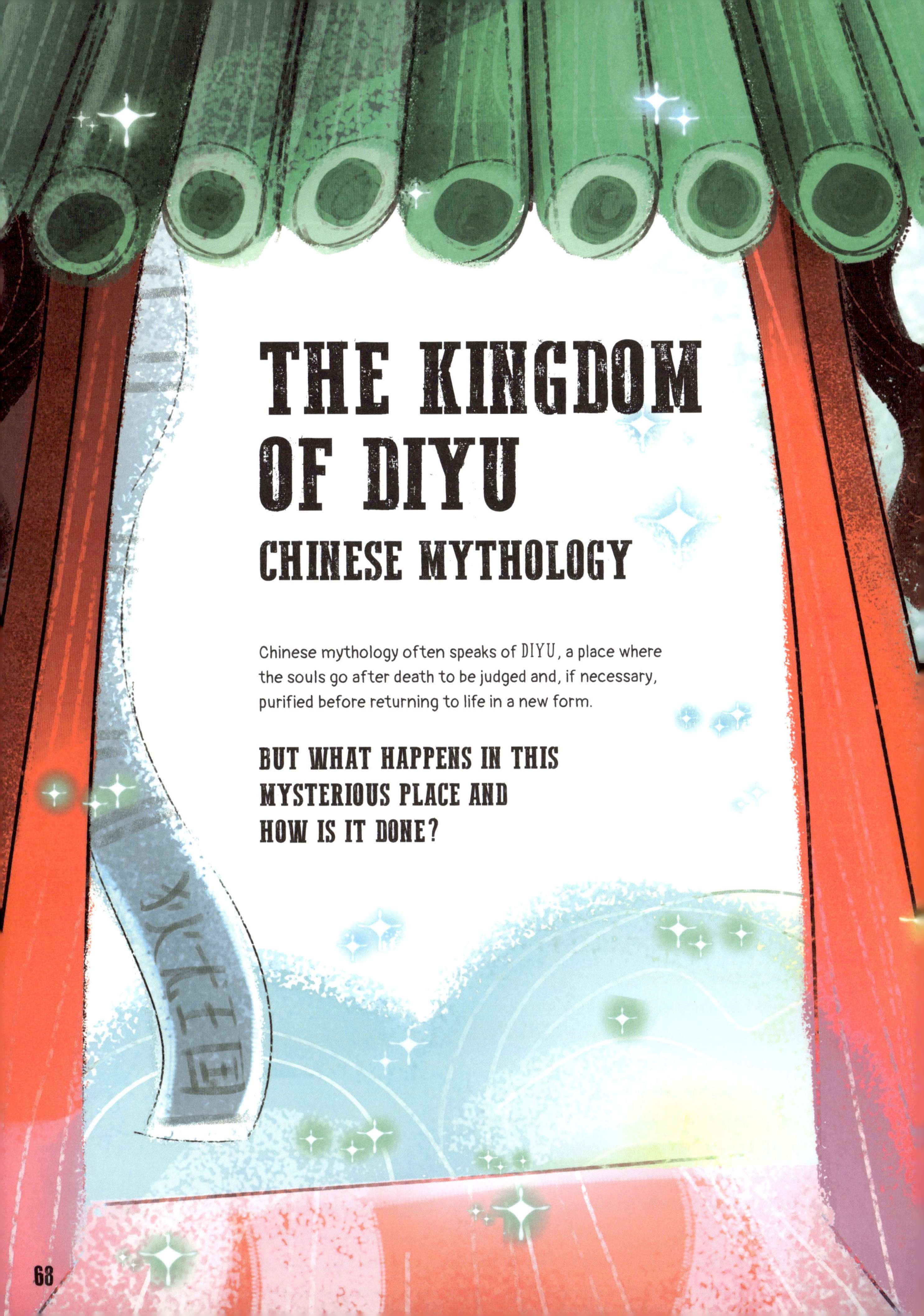

THE KINGDOM OF DIYU

CHINESE MYTHOLOGY

Chinese mythology often speaks of DIYU, a place where the souls go after death to be judged and, if necessary, purified before returning to life in a new form.

BUT WHAT HAPPENS IN THIS MYSTERIOUS PLACE AND HOW IS IT DONE?

You have to know that DIYU is an underground kingdom where those arriving in the afterlife must face judges and tests. It resembles a large court that is divided into ten smaller courts, each of which is governed by a special judge. Every court has its own task, and each judge must decide what will happen to the new arrivals.

CERTAINLY YOU WILL WANT TO KNOW MORE ABOUT THESE COURTS? YES? HERE IS SOME INFORMATION FOR YOU:

The ten courts of DIYU are like rooms of an enormous underground palace, and each one is different from the other. Every time a soul arrives in a court they must face a test depending on their actions in life. If the person was good, they will be able to pass easily, but if they have done bad things, they must face various punishments to find the right road again.

YANLUO WANG AND THE JUDGES

Now that I have told you about the ten courts, you will certainly be asking yourself who the judges are that handle the new arrivals to DIYU.

The most powerful of all is YANLUO WANG, the king of the Kingdom of the Dead. He presides over the first court, where all the souls go to be judged.

IF ANY OF THEM ARE REALLY BAD, THEY COULD BE SENT TO ANOTHER COURT, WHERE THEY WILL UNDERGO VERY HARD PUNISHMENTS.

Then there are also the other judges, like CHI JIANG WANG, who is responsible for the second court and judges those who have very serious sins, and SONG DI WANG. Every judge has their specific task and a series of rules to follow.

BUT THAT IS NOT ALL!

In the world of DIYU, in addition to the judges, there are also various demons and ghosts that work to carry out the sentences. These guardians are truly frightening and help to punish those who did ill, but not all of them are bad!

MANY JUST HAVE TO PASS THROUGH THE COURTS TO BE PURIFIED, AS IF TAKING A LOVELY PERFUMED BATH TO CLEAN THEMSELVES PROPERLY AND PREPARE TO RETURN TO THE WORLD.

THE MYTH OF REBIRTH

Once the souls that have arrived in DIYU have been judged and purified, YANLUO WANG or other judges decide what will happen to them. If the soul behaved quite well, they may come back to life in a new body.

In this way, life continues in an infinite cycle.

TIAN, which is the sky, is a little like the "great planner" who decides when a soul is ready to return to life in another body, in order to learn to grow more.

BUT HOW DOES REBIRTH WORK?

Imagine that the souls who were good during their lives are rewarded with a new opportunity to do good in the world, maybe as new people, animals, or even plants! However, if they have done bad things, they must stay longer in the kingdom of DIYU to improve more before being able to be reborn.

THIS MYTH TEACHES US THAT THE ACTIONS THAT WE DO DURING OUR LIFETIME HAVE CONSEQUENCES. BUT EVEN IF WE MAKE A MISTAKE, WE CAN ALWAYS TRY TO DO BETTER.

IT IS A NICE MESSAGE, RIGHT?

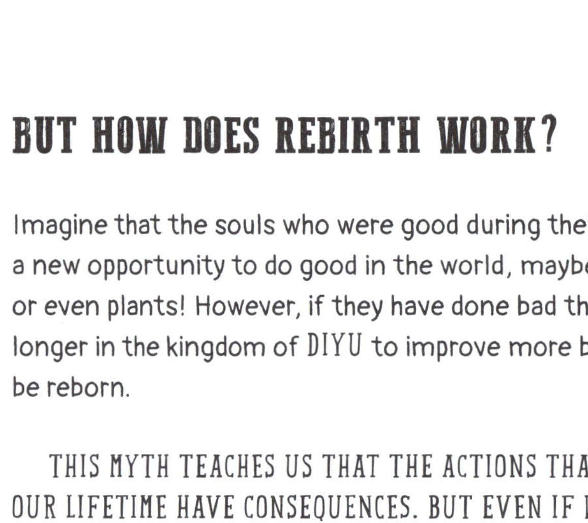

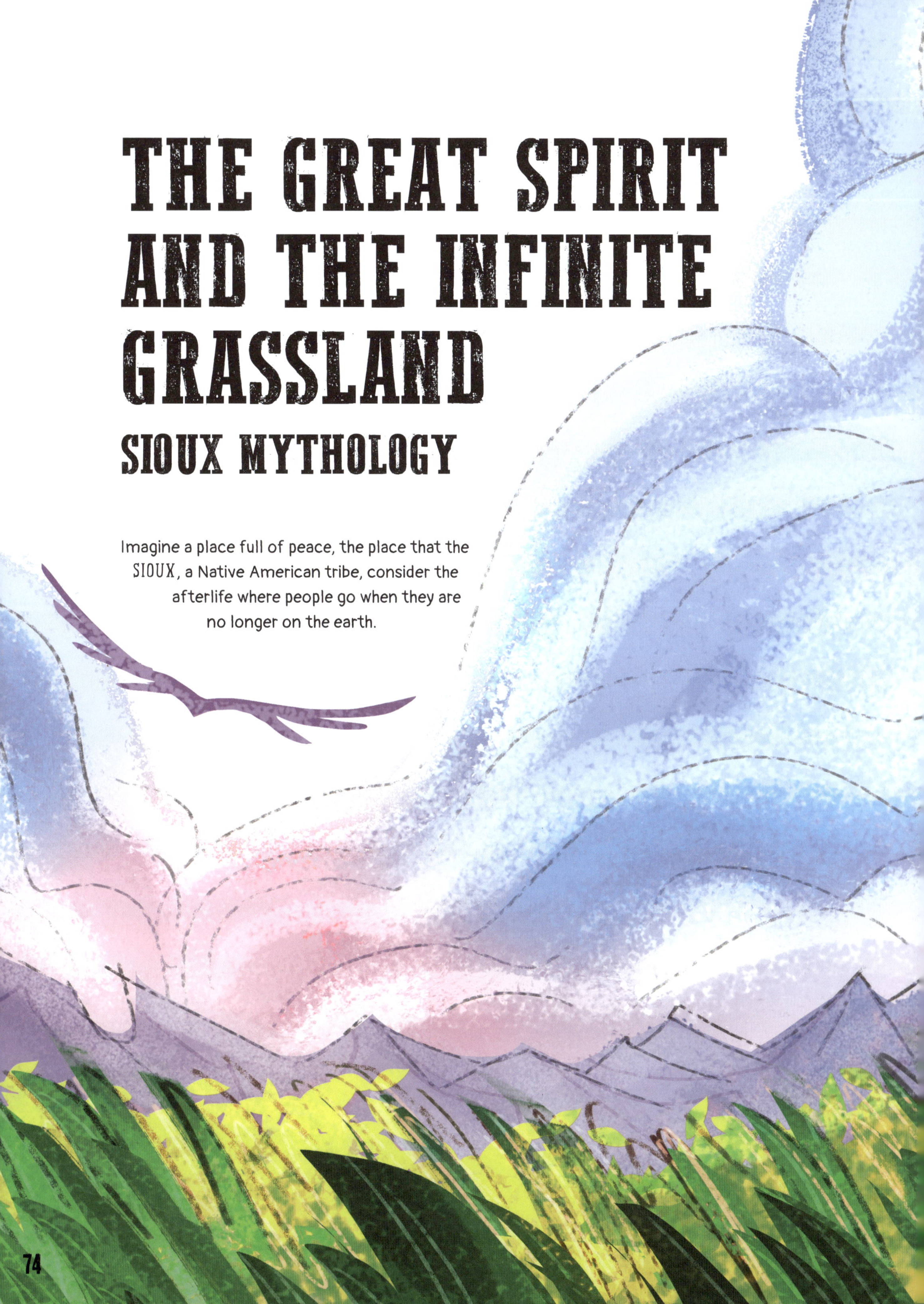

THE GREAT SPIRIT AND THE INFINITE GRASSLAND

SIOUX MYTHOLOGY

Imagine a place full of peace, the place that the SIOUX, a Native American tribe, consider the afterlife where people go when they are no longer on the earth.

For the SIOUX, life never really ends. When a person dies, they do not go away forever but enter a special world, called the GREAT INFINITE GRASSLAND. Here, the sky is always blue, the wind blows gently, and the animals run free.

The GREAT SPIRIT, who is a very powerful, good force, guides everyone on this voyage. Thanks to it, the people are never really alone because nature, the animals, and the stars continue to be with them. So, even if their bodies are no longer here, their spirits live forever.

THE SIOUX BELIEVE THAT IN THIS WORLD LIFE IS A CYCLE, SIMILAR TO A RIVER THAN NEVER STOPS FLOWING, AND EVERY TIME THEY LOOK AT THE SKY OR SEE AN ANIMAL RUNNING FAST, THEY FEEL THAT THEIR LOVED ONES ARE THERE WITH THEM, HAPPY AND ETERNALLY AT PEACE.

WAKAN TANKA AND THE FOUR SUPERIOR SPIRITS

WAKAN TANKA is the name that the SIOUX give to a very great and special power. It is everything that exists: the sky, the earth, the animals, the plants, and even the people. It is the energy that makes everything move and happen in the universe.

In fact, the SIOUX believe that WAKAN TANKA created the world from nothing. First it created the sky, then the earth, and last, the animals and the plants, putting everything in its place in perfect harmony.

WAKAN TANKA, HOWEVER, IS NOT ALONE: IT ALSO HAS SOME HELPERS CALLED THE FOUR SUPERIOR SPIRITS, EACH OF WHICH HAS A SPECIAL TASK TO MAINTAIN THE EQUILIBRIUM OF THE WORLD.

They are TUNKASHILA, the eldest and wisest, the protector of the family and traditions.

Then there is IKTOMI, the SPIRIT OF THE SPIDER, who helps people learn from their errors.

The third is PTEHINCALA, the SPIRIT OF THE ANTELOPE, who helps the earth to stay alive and moving.

Last, there is WI, the SPIRIT OF THE SUN, who illuminates everything with its light, bringing life and growth.

THE SPIRIT OF THE BISON, THE SPIRIT OF THE BEAR, THE FOUR WINDS, AND THE WHIRLWIND

I have told you about the superior spirits that help WAKAN TANKA, but you must know that for the SIOUX many more exist.

Among these we can't forget the SPIRIT OF THE BISON, who protects the grasslands and guarantees that no one goes hungry.

Then there is the SPIRIT OF THE BEAR, who helps those who need courage and resistance.

In addition, there are the FOUR WINDS: the WIND OF THE NORTH, which brings freshness and winter, the WIND OF THE EAST, which brings the dawn and hope, the WIND OF THE SOUTH, which brings the heat of summer, and the WIND OF THE WEST, which brings the calm of the evening.

EACH IS IMPORTANT TO MAINTAIN BALANCE IN THE WORLD.

Last, there is the WHIRLWIND, a strong and impetuous spirit that sends an important message: When everything seems overwhelmed by the storm, a moment of calm always comes.

ILLUSTRATOR

Isabella Ceravolo is an established illustrator, concept designer, and character designer with a background in animation cinema at the Nemo Academy. Her freelance work showcases her creative talent in books, fashion design, and animation. Isabella's illustrations are known for their vibrant and imaginative quality, making complex myths accessible and engaging.

AUTHOR

Since she was a child, Tea Orsi has adored inventing stories, writing and even illustrating them with small drawings in vivid colors. As the years have passed, her passion for writing has never faded. Today, she is a screenwriter of animated series and the author of comics, books, and magazines for children. She spends her day in the company of princesses, fairies, and other fantastic characters, always ready to live new, fun adventures on television and printed pages. She lives in Parma, Italy, with her family and two lovely little dogs, and loves traveling around the world in search of ideas and details that can inspire new stories all still to be told.

Piazzale Luigi Cadorna, 6 - 20123 Milan, Italy
www.whitestar.it

Translation: Qontent
Editing: Michele Suchomel-Casey

First printing, August 2025

ISBN 978-88-544-2165-3
1 2 3 4 5 6   29 28 27 26 25

Printed and manufactured in Turkey
by Arkadas Printhouse
Ankara Turkey